It's time for action.
COWS IN ACTION!

Genius cow Professor McMoo and
his trusty sidekicks, Pat and Bo,
are star agents of the C.I.A.
– short for COWS IN ACTION!
They travel through time, fighting
evil bulls from the future and
keeping history on the right track . . .

Find out more at
www.**cows**inaction.com

Read all the adventures of McMoo, Pat and Bo:

Coming soon!

THE VIKING EMOO-GENCY

www.cowsinaction.com

Also by Steve Cole:

ASTROSAURS

Coming soon!

ASTROSAURS ACADEMY

www.astrosaurs.co.uk

FIRST COWS ON THE MOOON

Steve Cole

Illustrated by Woody Fox

RED FOX

FIRST COWS ON THE MOOON
A RED FOX BOOK 978 1 849 41396 1

First published in Great Britain by Red Fox,
an imprint of Random House Children's Books
A Random House Group Company

This edition published 2011

1 3 5 7 9 10 8 6 4 2

The Random House Group Limited supports the Forest Stewardship
Council (FSC), the leading international forest certification organization.
All our titles that are printed on Greenpeace-approved FSC-certified paper
carry the FSC logo. Our paper procurement policy can be found at
www.randomhouse.co.uk/environment.

Mixed Sources
Product group from well-managed
forests and other controlled sources
www.fsc.org Cert no. TT-COC-2139
© 1996 Forest Stewardship Council

Set in 16/20pt Bembo Schoolbook

Red Fox Books are published by Random House Children's Books,
61–63 Uxbridge Road, London W5 5SA

www.**kids**at**randomhouse**.co.uk
www.**randomhouse**.co.uk

Addresses for companies within The Random House Group Limited
can be found at: www.randomhouse.co.uk/offices.htm

THE RANDOM HOUSE GROUP
Limited Reg. No. 954009

A CIP catalogue record for this book is available
from the British Library.

Printed and bound in Great Britain by
CPI Bookmarque, Croydon CR0 4TD

For Captain Denis Dallaire, US Air Force –
technical advisor, brother-in-law and friend

★ THE C.I.A. FILES ★

Cows from the present —
Fighting in the past to protect the future . . .

In the year 2550, after thousands of years of being eaten and milked, cows finally live as equals with humans in their own country of Luckyburger. But a group of evil war-loving bulls — the Fed-up Bull Institute — is not satisfied.

Using time machines and deadly ter-moo-nator agents, the F.B.I. is trying to change Earth's history. These bulls plan to enslave all humans and put savage cows in charge of the planet. Their actions threaten to plunge all cowkind into cruel and cowardly chaos . . .

The C.I.A. was set up to stop them.

However, the best agents come not from 2550 — but from the present. From a time in the early 21st century, when the first clever cows began to appear. A time when a brainy bull named Angus McMoo invented the first time machine, little realizing he would soon become the F.B.I.'s number one enemy . . .

COWS OF COURAGE —
TOP SECRET FILES

PROFESSOR ANGUS MCMOO

Security rating: Bravo Moo Zero

Stand-out features: Large white squares on coat, outstanding horns

Character: Scatterbrained, inventive, plucky and keen

Likes: Hot tea, history books, gadgets

Hates: Injustice, suffering, poor-quality tea bags

Ambition: To invent the electric sundial

LITTLE BO VINE

Security rating: For your cow pies only

Stand-out features: Luminous udder (colour varies)

Character: Tough, cheeky, ready-for-anything rebel

Likes: Fashion, chewing gum, self-defence classes

Hates: Bessie Barmer, the farmer's wife

Ambition: To run her own martial arts club for farmyard animals

PAT VINE

Security rating: Licence to fill (stomach with grass)

Stand-out features: Zigzags on coat

Character: Brave, loyal and practical

Likes: Solving problems, anything Professor McMoo does

Hates: Flies not easily swished by his tail

Ambition: To find a five-leaf clover — and to survive his dangerous missions!

Prof. McMoo's
TIMELINE OF NOTABLE
HISTORICAL EVENTS

4.6 billion years BC
PLANET EARTH FORMS
(good job too)

13.7 billion years BC
BIG BANG – UNIVERSE BEGINS
(and first tea atoms created)

23 million years BC
FIRST COWS APPEAR

(23 million is my lucky number!)

1700 BC
SHEN NUNG MAKES FIRST CUP OF TEA
(what a hero!)

7000 BC
FIRST CATTLE KEPT ON FARMS
(Not a great year for cows)

1901 AD
QUEEN VICTORIA DIES
(she was not a-moo-sed)

2550 BC
GREAT PYRAMID BUILT AT GIZA
(by an Egyptian geezer!)

31 BC ROMAN EMPIRE FOUNDED

(Ruum-Moo empire founded by a cow but no one remembers that)

1509 AD HENRY VIII COMES TO THE THRONE

(and probably squashes it)

1066 AD BATTLE OF HASTINGS

('but what about the Cattle of Hastings?)

1620 AD ENGLISH PILGRIMS SETTLE IN AMERICA

(bringing with them the first cows to moo in an American accent)

1939 AD WORLD WAR TWO BEGINS

(or World War Moo as its known to cows)

2007 AD I INVENT A TIME MACHINE!!!

2500 AD COW NATION OF LUCKYBURGER FOUNDED

(HOORAY!)

(about time!)

1903 AD FIRST TEABAGS INVENTED

2550 AD COWS IN ACTION RECRUIT PROFESSOR McMOO, PAT AND BO

(and now the fun REALLY starts...)

FIRST COWS ON THE MOOON

Chapter One

UFO OR MOO-FO?

The moon was full and silver-bright over Farmer Barmer's organic farm. Most of the animals were sound asleep in barns or pens or sties. But one young bullock called Pat Vine was wide-awake in his field, peering up at the stars through a homemade telescope.

"Star-gazing's amazing!" he murmured. "I can see the Big Dipper!"

"You *are* a big dipper," came a voice behind him.

Pat turned to see his big sister smiling cheekily at him. "Hello, Little Bo," he said – then noticed her udder was glowing bright yellow. "What happened to you?"

"I found some luminous paint in a barn," Bo explained. "I thought I'd slap some on to light my way when I sneak out for my nightly kickboxing practice. After all, if anyone found me holding a torch, they might suspect that I'm no ordinary cow."

Pat frowned. "How many ordinary

cows have luminous udders?"

"I don't know, I never look — a cow's udder is her own business." Bo folded her arms. "Anyway, how many ordinary bullocks own a telescope?"

"It's not mine," said Pat. "I borrowed it from the professor. He made it himself — isn't he brilliant?"

"Yep," Bo agreed. "Or brilliantly barmy, anyway!"

Pat smiled. Professor Angus McMoo was the brainiest bull in the world — and, most likely, in all the other worlds you could spot through his telescope. McMoo, Pat and Bo were Emmsy-Squares, a rare breed of very clever cattle. But that wasn't the only extraordinary thing about them . . .

Bo shoved Pat out of the way and squinted through the 'scope. "I suppose the moon *is* pretty cool. How does that old human song go? *Hey diddle diddle, the bull did a widdle . . .*"

"He did not!" The burly, red–brown figure of Professor McMoo burst out of his nearby shed. "Or if he did, he certainly washed his hooves afterwards." With a grin he straightened his spectacles. "I think you'll find it's: *Hey diddle diddle, the cat and the fiddle . . .*"

"*The cow jumped over the moon*," Pat remembered with a smile. "Oh, wouldn't it be amazing to go up into space?"

"It would be a good laugh," Bo said. "If you were really smart, Professor, you'd have turned your shed into a spaceship – not a rickety old time machine!"

"Oi!" McMoo frowned. "That 'rickety old time machine' of mine can whizz you anywhere on the planet, into the past, present or future – isn't that out-of-this-world enough for you?"

"It certainly is," said Pat loyally.

"I suppose so," agreed Bo. "After all, if the Time Shed was a Space Shed, we'd never have joined the Cows In Action!"

Pat could hardly remember life before the crime-busting, *time*-busting C.I.A. had travelled back from the future and asked the clever cows to join their fight against the F.B.I. – the Fed-up Bull Institute. Although in the twenty-sixth century cows lived as equals with humans, these villainous bulls were always trying to change history and start a new age of dia-*bull*-ical tyranny over cows and humans alike. And so McMoo, Pat and Bo had agreed to postpone the carefree tour through time they had planned, and join the C.I.A.'s ranks instead.

"That's funny," the professor said suddenly. "I thought I saw something shimmying past the moon . . ." He peered through the telescope. "I wonder . . . could it have been a UFO?"

"A what?" asked Bo.

"An Unidentified Flying Object," McMoo explained, giving the telescope to Bo. "A flying saucer. An alien spaceship."

Pat gulped. "Aliens? Flying past the moon?"

"Yeah, very likely." Bo turned the telescope towards the farmhouse. "Ugh, this thing should come with a health warning, Prof! I just got a big-time close-up view of Bessie Barmer and her mum!"

Pat shuddered. Bessie was Farmer Barmer's wife, a fearsome fatty who hated all the livestock. For the last week

she'd had her mum Gertie staying, on
a visit from America. It had not been a
pleasant time. By day the farmyard
resounded with the two women's
heavy footsteps and mocking voices,
and by night it shook with their mean
laughter.

"I overheard Bessie telling Farmer
Barmer she was going to spring a surprise
on her mother tonight," said McMoo
thoughtfully. "I wonder what . . ."

"We can spy on them!" Bo suggested,
giving the telescope to Pat. "They're
gassing away in the front room right
now."

Pat pressed his eye to the eyepiece and
gasped as he saw Gertie up close. She was
twice as old as her daughter
and three times as hefty.
And by reading their
lips he could tell
what the two nasty
ladies were saying.

"Oh, *no*!" he cried, almost dropping the telescope. "Gertie just told Bessie she likes it here so much she wants to stay for ever!" More spiteful chuckles came out of the farmhouse. "And . . . Bessie just said she'll knock down *our* shed to build Gertie a cottage!"

"No way!" Bo groaned. "I know Bessie's a pain in the butt, but I love living here on the farm."

"Professor," asked Pat, "what can we do? I don't want to move!"

"You might change your tune," said McMoo grimly, still staring up into the night sky. "Give me that telescope . . ."

Pat passed it to the professor, then peered at the stars too. Even with the naked eye he could see a bright dot growing slowly larger. "Is it a spaceship, Professor?"

"Yes." McMoo passed him the telescope. "And it's headed our way!"

Pat gasped as he saw a spinning disc,

bristling with guns
and covered with
thick black and
white splodges.
"It's . . . patterned
like cow hide!"

"Let me see!" Bo
snatched the 'scope and saw it for herself.
"You're right. Never mind your UFO,
Prof – that thing is a *Moo*-FO!"

With a sudden surge
of speed the unlikely
object swooped into
clear sight overhead.
Bo stared up, petrified.
"There . . . there's
writing on
that thing."

"*F.B.I. Space Patrol*,"
McMoo read, sounding grave. "Looks
like our enemies have changed tactics.
Instead of travelling through time to get
us, they've journeyed across the stars!"

"And there are more Moo-FOs on the way! Look!"

Pat tried not to quiver as more of the spinning, cow-coloured saucers came hurtling out of the starry darkness.

Then, suddenly, two towering, battle-

scarred bull-creatures jumped out of the nearest spaceship and crashed down to earth. They were clad in ragged red spacesuits and dented armour. Green eyes glowed behind blank metal masks, and sabre-sharp horns stuck out of their round glass space helmets. One wore a heavy-duty laser gun on his left wrist.

McMoo nodded grimly at the gruesome figures. "Well, well. Two of the F.B.I.'s most deadly agents – ter-moo-nators!"

"We have come to destroy you," said the larger of the two monsters in a mechanical voice. "The humans of this planet are finally doomed – and so are the three of you!"

Chapter Two

DOUBLE THE TROUBLE

McMoo eyed the sinister cow-ships gathering in the sky and took a deep breath. "Well, this is charming," he said mildly to the two ter-moo-nators. "But, please, won't you introduce yourselves before you blast us into oxtail soup?"

"You pretend not to know us?" rasped the smaller one. "You do not recognize T-312, your old enemy?"

"And me, the deadly T-207?" droned the other.

"Nope," the professor admitted. "I've never seen either of you before in my life. Perhaps your memory-banks have blown a fuse . . ."

T–207's eyes glowed brighter. "Negative."

"We have spent decades in the darkness of space, longing to destroy you," said T–312, raising his gun. "And finally, the time has come—"

"Watch it, Professor!" Pat hurled himself at McMoo, knocking him clear, just as a blast of laser-light shot from the gun. *KA-ZAMMM!* A fence behind him exploded in flames.

At the same time, Bo punched T-312 with all her strength and sent him staggering into T-207. Both robo-bulls collapsed in a heap.

"Thanks," McMoo told his friends as Pat helped him up. "I was very nearly flame-grilled!"

"Quick!" cried Bo. "Retreat to the Time Shed."

"So we can contact the C.I.A. for help?" McMoo frowned. "That's a very sensible idea — not like you at all."

"You don't understand." Bo pointed to the farmhouse. "Bessie and Gertie are coming outside — and I can't fight when I'm feeling completely sick!"

Pat and McMoo turned to see the whopping, sour-faced ratbags stomping outside.

"What's all this racket?" Bessie hollered — then took in the ter-moo-nators and their Moo-FO. "*Eeeeek!* Look —

14

metal bulls from outer space!"

Gertie Barmer's crinkled face screwed up in a frown. "Aww, no way! It can't be . . ."

The ter-moo-nators swung round stiffly at the interruption and fired their death rays at the Barmers. The wall behind the women blew up in a hail of stone and sparks. "*Oww!*" Bessie hollered as she and Gertie dived behind a trough for cover. "Those bricks hit my bum!"

"They could hardly miss," Pat commented.

"Come on, while those robo-bulls are distracted," McMoo yelled. "Leg it!"

The three Cows In Action pounded over to the shelter of the professor's barn. But as they approached, a creaking, grinding sound started up from within.

McMoo skidded to a stop in shock. "Someone's powering up the Time Shed!"

Pat ran on ahead with Bo. "Perhaps it's one of our C.I.A. friends from the future, come to lend a helping hoof."

Bo kicked open the door – and

gasped. "Nice thought, little bruv – but dead wrong."

Ordinarily, Pat's eyes would be drawn to the transformation of the shed as it switched from grotty outbuilding to super-incredible time machine – the way hidden systems in the walls spun round into sight, and a huge, horseshoe-shaped bank of controls slid up from the ground in the middle. But right now his attention was fixed on the two terrifying, robotic bull-creatures turning to face him.

"Oh, no," groaned McMoo, following his friends inside. "*More* ter-moo-nators!"

Pat stood his ground and studied the new arrivals. They looked just the same as the monsters outside, except they weren't wearing space helmets and their armour was gleaming, with not a scratch to be seen. Branded on their burnished bronze breastplates were familiar numbers . . .

"Professor!" Bo gasped. "These tin-heads are called T-207 and T-312 – just like the ter-moo-nators outside!"

"What's going on?" McMoo demanded.

"Silence," rasped T-312 as T-207 started dismantling the banks of controls. "How dare you interrupt us while we are stealing your technology."

"You are *not*," said McMoo. "It took me years to pinch that stuff from the bins of the scientist next door . . . you can't just—"

"SILENCE." T-312 raised his gun and fired at the three agents. McMoo pushed his friends behind a hay bale as the death ray zapped past and blew up a control panel. The ter-moo-nator fired again, and the ground at McMoo's hooves erupted in molten mud, hurling him backwards.

Pat peeped out from behind a hay bale. "How come you're called the same as the ter-moo-nators outside?" he demanded. "You even look the same."

"This data does not compute," T-312 snarled. "No two ter-moo-nators have the same number. And we have not been outside – our portable F.B.I. time machine brought us straight into this shed."

As he spoke, T-207 yanked a piece of equipment and a bright yellow lever

clean out of the console in a spray of sparks. Then he smashed his steel hoof down on a microphone beside it.

"That does it!" yelled Bo. She somersaulted over the haystack in *kung moo* mode and tried kicking T-207 in the tum. But the

ter-moo-nator batted her away, and
T-312 fired his heavy-duty hoof blaster
once more. Bo dived for cover as the
laser struck the shed doors, knocking
them open – to reveal the two scuffed
and battered ter-moo-nators still
standing there.

Pat stared. "How can those tin-heads
be out there *and* in here at the same
time?"

"They must be from two different
times!" McMoo realized, struggling to
his hooves. "That's why the ter-moo-
nators outside know us: they're *older*

versions of the ter-moo-nators in here."

"My brain hurts just thinking about it," Bo complained. "But look – the younger ones are pushing off!"

Still holding the battered metal box with the yellow lever attached, the two shiny ter-moo-nators had hopped onto their time transporter – a large silver platter – and were already fading away. "Objectives achieved," warbled T-207, his mechanical tones lingering in the air. "Proceeding to the past to complete our mission . . ."

"Quick, Bo – close the doors before those old timers can get inside." McMoo ran over to the scorched controls and sighed. "Great. The communicator's been zapped – now we can't even call the C.I.A. for help!"

Bo jammed the smoking doors shut. "So what *can* we do?"

"Well," said the professor, "the drive

systems are still working – we'd better get going."

"We can't just leave the world to be destroyed by killer cows and push off to another time!" cried Bo.

"We must," said McMoo grimly. "With the C.I.A. out of contact, the only way we can foil this crazy invasion is to track those ter-moo-nators through time and stop them from starting it in the first place."

Pat gulped. "But their attack is already happening, right now. I thought it was really dangerous to try to change history?"

"It is. But we have no choice." McMoo yanked down hard on the take-off lever. "To protect the future we must alter the past – or else the Fed-up Bull Institute will conquer the world!"

Chapter Three

JOURNEY TO THE SPACE CENTRE OF THE EARTH

As the Time Shed rocked and wobbled on the seas of Earth's history, Pat and Bo sat miserably on a haystack. They watched the professor busily fiddling with his controls, trying to get an exact fix on the ter-moo-nator thieves.

"I've never seen him look so serious," said Pat.

"He must have a lot on his mind," replied Bo. "I forgot to put any milk and sugar in his tea. Or any hot water.

24

Or any tea bags. And he still drank it without saying thank you."

Pat frowned. "There wasn't a whole lot to thank you for, was there?"

"At least the bucket was clean," Bo protested.

"Found them!" cried McMoo suddenly. "The Kennedy Space Centre, Florida, USA, in the year 1969." He turned to the special TV screen hanging down from the rafters. "Computer – tell us more . . ."

The computer calmly obeyed.

++ Kennedy Space Centre ++ Constructed in 1963 during the "space race" between America and Russia ++ A springboard for sending satellites and rockets into space ++ It covered an area of land 34 miles long and 6 miles wide ++ The *Apollo* moon missions – America's £8,000 million spaceflight programme – were all launched from this "moonport" using vast Saturn V rockets and specially built launch pads ++ In July 1969 *Apollo 11* took the first human beings to the moon and brought them safely back again – an incredible technological feat ++

"It's the ter-moo-nators' technological *feet* I'm worried about," Bo declared.

"Then you should worry about them visiting a space centre. Those rusty robo-bulls attacked us in spaceships, remember?" Pat turned to McMoo. "What was that about a space race?"

"America and Russia were fierce enemies back then," the professor explained. "Both countries built enough weapons to destroy the world, and came close to using them on several occasions."

Bo sighed. "Humans are so stupid."

"Each side wanted to prove they were strongest and smartest," McMoo went on. "So the race to put men on the moon kicked off – and in the end, America won." He paused, looking at the controls. "According to my time scanner, those ter-moo-nators have travelled back to May the eighteenth 1969, just a couple of months before the first moon landing."

"I wonder what they're up to," said

26

Pat. "What was that yellow lever and the box they took, Professor?"

"The ZEN-generator," McMoo told him. "ZEN stands for Zone of Extra Nothingness." He patted the horseshoe-shaped bank of controls. "It's where this little beauty goes when I turn off the Time Shed."

"I thought it just sank into the ground," said Bo.

"And get all mucky?" McMoo looked appalled. "What kind of crazy genius inventor do you take me for? No, no, the ZEN-generator creates a zone of extra nothingness – a kind of magic hole – for the console to disappear into until I call it out again. Much tidier." He frowned. "But in the hooves of the ter-moo-nators, that generator could be dangerous."

Bo nodded. "They could clobber someone with it."

"Or more likely use it to change history somehow," said Pat.

"Whatever," said Bo. "Look, Prof, if we're going to this space base, we'll need to fit in with the humans. You'd better bring out the ringblenders."

"Good point." McMoo quickly went over to a small cupboard and pulled out a silver ring for each of them. Pat took the clever C.I.A. gadget gratefully. When worn through the nose, ringblenders created an optical illusion that disguised cattle as people – so long as they wore the right clothes.

"What are we going to wear, then?" asked Bo. "Anything funky?"

McMoo was already rifling through his special costume cupboard. "There are two US air bases near the Kennedy Space Centre," he said. "So let's pretend to be a group of high-ranking officers

come for a look-see . . ." He chucked
over a couple of uniforms and pulled out
a third for himself. "Computer – forge us
some ID and a cover story, could you?
Might come in handy . . ."

While the computer creaked and
whirred and got busy printing, Pat
struggled into his dark blue braided
uniform. Then he pushed in his ringblender and checked his reflection in the
Time Shed's special
mirror. It showed him as
a handsome young
officer.

Bo pushed him
aside and
surveyed her
own
uniformed
appearance
with less
enthusiasm.
"This look is

rubbish. How about I tear some holes in it and set it off with a pink crocodile-skin apron?"

"I don't think so," said McMoo, pulling a peaked cap over his horns. His smart blazer bore strips of colourful squares to show off his high rank. "Now, then . . ." The shed suddenly rattled and clunked – a sound like a hundred milkcrates falling from a great height. "We've landed. Let's get out there and start stopping those ter-moo-nators, shall we?"

Pat smiled bravely and nodded. But he knew that the professor's cheeriness was only an act. With their home under attack in the future, and with no way to call on the C.I.A. for help, things had seldom seemed so desperate.

Bo threw open the doors. Outside, the day was warm and bright, and the sunlight glinted on dozens of fenced-off huts and workshops all across the sprawling space base. Towering in the distance was something that looked like a massive white missile attached to an even taller framework of red crisscrossed steel.

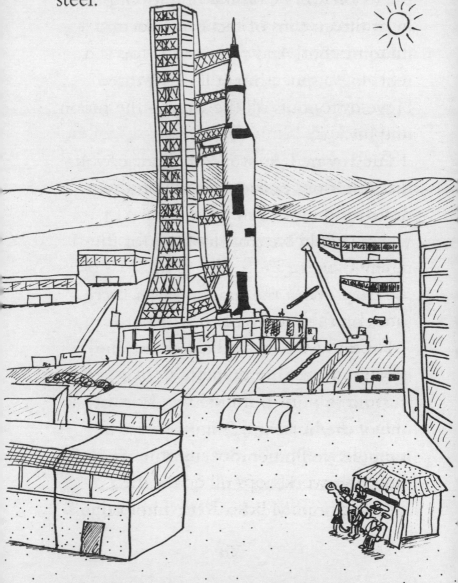

"Wow!" McMoo beamed and rubbed his hooves together. "A Saturn V rocket, just like the computer said. It's twice as tall as Nelson's Column and its engines burn fifteen tons of fuel every second – imagine that! And right at the top is a real *Apollo* spaceship. It'll carry three brave astronauts all the way to the moon and back . . ."

Pat frowned. As was so often the way, the professor's passion for the past was distracting him from his mission. "Er, where should we start looking for the ter-moo-nators?"

"How about the building over there that's on fire?" asked Bo.

Pat and McMoo looked where she was pointing. Sure enough, smoke was starting to pour from the windows of one of the huts. Suddenly, a figure in a protective flameproof suit ran out from behind a bunker.

"Aha," said McMoo. "It's a hot papa!"

Bo frowned. "A *what* papa?"

"The firefighters on this base are called 'hot papas' because when rocket fuel catches fire, things get *very* hot indeed," McMoo explained. "He'll soon have this piffling blaze under control."

"Or not," said Pat. "Look, he's run straight past!"

"Well, if he's not going to bother putting out that fire – I will!" Bo rushed up to the smoking hut, hitched up her uniform and put out the flames with a long *sloosh* of milk from her luminous udder. "There – it takes a cow to do a man's work."

"I don't think that *was* a man, Bo," said McMoo grimly. "I saw horns poking through his flame-proof mask . . ."

Pat gulped. "It must be one of the ter-moo-nators!"

McMoo ran over to a fire alarm mounted on a nearby wall and whacked it. At once, a warning siren shrieked out across the space centre. "Come on – he went that-a-way. Let's get after him!"

The valiant cattle raced across the grass towards a group of concrete storerooms. The door on one had been wrenched off its hinges. McMoo led the charge and pushed his way inside . . .

Where the suited figure stood on the

other side of the room, sweeping electronic components off a shelf and stuffing them in his pockets. The twin points poking up through his headgear were plain to see.

McMoo cleared his throat noisily, and the intruder swung round. "You know, most staff members would get the sack for what you're doing."

"But don't worry – *you're* going to get the PUNCH!" Bo jumped onto a workbench and dived towards the startled thief. "Hey, hot papa – come to milky mama!"

SLAMMM! Bo pushed him into the shelves, which toppled and collapsed with a terrific crash. The figure gave a moo of alarm as its protective helmet fell away . . .

To reveal the big brown eyes of a frightened young calf!

Chapter Four

SECURITY SHOCKS

"Hey, what's the big idea?" Bo stared down at the calf in puzzlement. "I was expecting someone I could beat up — not a helpless little kid."

"Kids grow up to be goats," growled the calf, seeming suddenly less scared as

his big eyes narrowed. "When I'm all grown I'll be a FED-UP BULL!"

So saying, he whacked Bo in the face with a surprisingly strong front hoof. She went tumbling over the workbench and crashed into Pat and the professor. Then, mooing fiercely, the calf tipped the heavy table on top of all three of them and sprinted for the door.

"Come back here!" Bo yelled from under the tabletop. "Cheeky little Herbert."

"The name's Dexter!" called the calf as he escaped. "And don't you forget it!"

Pat helped McMoo and Bo kick the workbench away. "I don't get it," he said, scrambling up. "Why would the F.B.I. use children as agents when they have ter-moo-nators?"

"Good question." McMoo dusted himself down. "Let's go and ask him!"

But by now their way was blocked. A huge and familiar woman had appeared in the doorway. She was panting like a dog and had a face like a dog's bottom,

and her lumpy, bumpy body was stuffed into the uniform of a security guard. "What the heck are you doing in here?" she bellowed in an American accent.

"Er . . ." Pat swallowed hard. "Is that who I think it is . . . ?"

Bo nodded grimly. "We saw her face through the telescope, and it almost broke the glass. It's Gertie, Bessie Barmer's mum – but more than forty years younger!"

"C'mon, spill the beans . . ." Gertie trailed off as she took in the high-ranking uniforms and gave an uncertain salute. "Um, sirs?"

McMoo puffed himself up. "That's better, Gertrude!"

"How did you know my name?" said Gertie.

"It's our business to know things," McMoo said sharply. "Now, if you'll excuse us, we have an intruder to chase. You just missed him."

"I didn't see nobody," Gertie growled.

Just then a large, worried-looking man in a dark suit burst into the room with a handful of sentries. "Miss Barmer? Why the alarms? Where's the fire?"

"We raised the alarm when we saw the fire in one of the supply huts," McMoo jumped in. "But don't worry – Lieutenant Bo Vine here put out the blaze single-handedly."

The big man frowned at Bo. "You did? Holy cow!"

"Holy's probably going a bit far," Bo said modestly, "but I am pretty impressive."

"Well, so am I, sister," the man replied. "I'm H. P. Blinkenshrink, director of this space centre." He glared at McMoo and Pat. "I think I'd better see some identification."

"Of course! I am Major-General Angus McMoo." The professor flashed his phoney pass. "Bo you know, and this is Lieutenant Pat Vine." He pulled a folded letter from his jacket pocket and passed it to Blinkenshrink.

"We've been sent by the President to perform a spot security check."

"But that doesn't include Gertie's spots," Bo said firmly.

Gertie scowled and stepped forward, but Blinkenshrink stopped her with a warning hand. "Holy smoke. This letter is signed by the President of the USA himself!" He smiled meekly at McMoo. "No one warned me you were coming to the space centre."

"Of course they didn't!" McMoo winked at his friends and spoke in confidential tones. "The President had concerns about security here and sent us along. And already we've seen an intruder dressed as a hot papa stealing from your stores."

"Hogwash!" snorted Gertie.

But suddenly, a young man dressed only in his boxer shorts staggered into the storeroom. Gertie, Blinkenshrink and the soldiers held their noses – the newcomer reeked of cow muck, and Pat noticed that his hair was thick with the stuff.

"Is *this* man a hot papa by any chance?" the professor enquired.

"He sure is, McMoo," Blinkenshrink admitted. "This is one of our top firefighters, Smoky Joe Jones. What happened to you, son?"

"It's obvious." Bo crouched down and placed a comforting arm around him. "Somebody's given you a pat on the head, right?"

"More like a wallop," said Smoky. "I was just patrolling down by the fuel store when something hit me from behind. I woke up in an empty garage with my uniform gone." He looked at the professor and frowned. "Did . . . Mr Blinkenshrink call you McMoo?"

"That's right," the professor agreed. "Major-General McMoo, as it happens."

Smoky looked at Pat and Bo. "And these are your friends?" When McMoo nodded, he smiled broadly. "Perhaps I could get you all a cup of tea?"

Blinkenshrink frowned. "We don't pay you to make tea, son!"

"It's a lovely offer," McMoo said quickly, "but while we stand here chewing the cud – er, chewing the fat, I mean – the thief is getting clean away."

Pat grimaced at the muck on Smoky's head. "Cleaner than his victim, for sure."

"All right, Barmer, get on the case," Blinkenshrink commanded. "Take your best guards and find that intruder."

"I'm coming too," cried Bo. "I owe him some lumps!"

"You'd better go with her, Pat," said McMoo. "You're good at finding things."

Pat saluted smartly and followed Gertie, Bo and the soldiers out of the room.

Smoky Joe lingered, still staring at McMoo. "*Please* let me get you a cup of tea . . ."

"I told you already," Blinkenshrink cried. "You're not the tea lady, for Pete's sake! Get out of here and clean yourself up!"

McMoo watched the firefighter hurry away and turned to the troubled director. "I'm guessing this isn't the first weird thing to happen around the space centre?"

"Lots of things have gone missing lately," Blinkenshrink confessed. "Electrical components, wiring, bits of metal . . . Little things, mostly, but they've just vanished without trace."

"Sounds to me like someone's trying to build something," McMoo reflected. "I wonder what . . . Surely with all the people working here and a security team on watch, a robber would be easy to catch?"

"No one's seen anything suspicious, up till now." Blinkenshrink scowled. "I bet it's the Russians, trying to steal our secrets!"

"I don't think it is," said McMoo quickly.

"They'd stop at nothing to damage

our space programme," the director went on. "It's bad news. Especially when we're launching *Apollo 10* this afternoon."

"Of course!" McMoo beamed. "It's a practice run, isn't it – they're going to test all the space gear on a flight around the moon, ahead of *Apollo 11* landing there in July . . ." He cleared his throat, trying to contain his excitement. "Er, anyway. Could I see a complete list of all the stolen bits and pieces?"

"Yup. I've got computer records over at the Launch Control Centre," said Blinkenshrink. "Why?"

"I'm hoping to work out what our mysterious thief wants to make," said McMoo. "And then I'm hoping to stop him!"

Pat and Bo sat in the back of an army Jeep as Gertie Barmer steered them all round the mammoth space centre, searching for any signs of the intruder.

Everywhere they went she questioned
firefighters, security officers and
puzzled scientists – but no one had
seen a thing.

"I wonder why Dexter the calf stole
a human uniform instead of wearing a
ringblender . . ." Pat pondered.

"Perhaps he's put one in by now," said Bo. "That's why these dumb humans can't see him."

Pat knew that only other cattle could see through a ringblender's optical illusion. "But if he had one," he argued, "why not wear it in the first place?"

Gertie stopped the Jeep beside a sentry hut. "Well, we've looked everywhere, and there's no sign of this intruder of yours. I bet he doesn't even exist."

"He attacked us!" Pat protested. "And look what happened to Smoky Joe."

"Aww, he probably just got socked by a frozen buffalo poo that fell out of a passing jet full of farm animals, and accidentally lost his uniform," said Gertie. "That's the likeliest explanation."

Bo shook her head. "There's one place we haven't looked yet." She pointed to the giant rocket on the launch pad. "There!"

Gertie's eyes bulged like a frog's. "You

think the intruder's on board *Apollo 10*?"

Pat smiled grimly. "There's only one way to find out!"

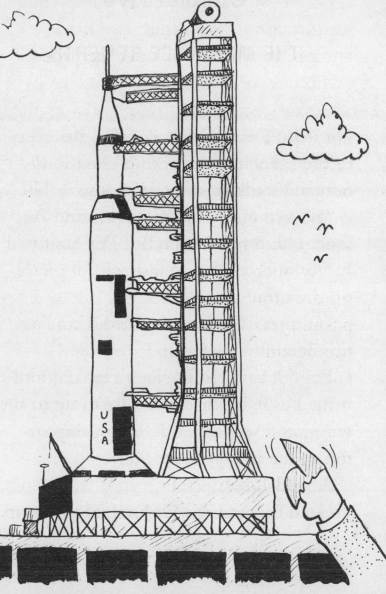

Chapter Five

THE MOO-NACE BENEATH

Grouchy Gertie drove Pat and Bo over to the launch pad, parking close to the Saturn V's impressive service tower. She clambered inside the metal lift and Bo squeezed in beside her. But Pat hesitated. He'd noticed some tiny specks of metal on the ground.

"C'mon," Gertie grumbled. "Let's get this craziness over with."

Pat got in the lift, which clanked and rattled as it slowly hauled them up to the command section of the moonship on top of the whopping rocket.

A wild-haired scientist in a white coat greeted them as the lift lurched to a stop.

"Hello," he said brightly.

Gertie grimaced in greeting. "Seen anything strange around here?"

"Why, no, ma'am," the boffin replied, gesturing to the empty spacecraft. "Everything's A-OK."

Gertie looked triumphant. "See?"

"I can see something," said Pat, pointing to the ground. "More tiny specks of metal . . ." He touched them – then snatched his hoof away. "Weird. They feel hot."

51

"It's a sunny day," said Gertie.

"I noticed some at the bottom of the service tower too," Pat persisted.

"Well . . ." Gertie nodded to the scientist. "He probably dropped them."

But the man shook his head. "Not me. Not much use for iron filings around here."

"Hey, what are these chalk marks on the outside of the spaceship?" Bo pointed to some neat little lines around the top and bottom of the craft.

"It looks like someone's been measuring it," said Pat slowly. He turned back to the scientist. "Are you sure you haven't seen anything suspicious?"

The boffin shook his head.

"Everything's A-OK," he repeated, and went back inside the cramped spaceship.

"You think some intruder sneaked through security just to drop some iron filings and measure this here spaceship?" Gertie scoffed. "You're plum crazy!"

"Nah," said Bo. "We hate plums."

"But we love clues." Pat studied the oddly hot iron filings. "And if these are nothing to do with the scientists and there are more back down at ground level . . ."

"They might just make a trail!" Bo grinned at her brother. "A trail leading someplace interesting. Let's check it out!"

Three miles away, McMoo was waiting in the Launch Control Centre for Blinkenshrink to produce his list of stolen components.

In barely twelve hours, *Apollo 10* would be launched from here, and the whole place was buzzing with activity.

Scores of seats were laid out in rows next to consoles full of monitors, scopes and switches, all of them facing large windows that gave them a perfect view of the launch pad.

"McMoo!" The director bustled up with a computer printout as big as a duvet. "Here you go – a complete list of everything that's gone missing."

"Hmm!" McMoo surveyed the lengthy list. "Did you consider getting a different security chief – one who knows what 'security' actually means?"

"I only promoted Barmer last week – after I'd sacked the previous three security chiefs for losing so much stuff." Blinkenshrink sighed. "It doesn't seem to matter who's in charge. For crying out loud, we've got guards and workers all around the site, and yet the thieves seem to come and go as they please. I just hope they don't steal anything else."

"Actually, I hope they *do*." McMoo looked at him grimly. "If not, it means they already have everything they need – and their plans can go ahead!"

Over by the rocket launch pad, Pat and Bo were hunting around for more of the mysterious iron filings, while Gertie Barmer watched impatiently.

"There's another few here," Pat reported, plucking a piece from the concrete. "Not far from this hatch in the ground."

55

Bo lifted the metal hatch cover. Beyond lay a stainless-steel chute, leading down into darkness. "Wonder where that leads?"

"It leads to a special room sixty metres underground," said Gertie. "The launch crew shoot down there if they think the rocket's about to blow up." She nodded to two sentries standing guard close by. "But this whole area is watched all the time. Right, boys?"

Both guards nodded. "Everything's A-OK," they said.

"Right," said Gertie. "So if you want

to waste your time scrabbling on the ground, Lieutenants, go ahead. But me, I've got better things to do – like, go on my coffee break!" And with that, she wobbled away.

Bo sighed. "That rotten old bat's not very helpful, is she? I bet she's working for the F.B.I."

"Maybe," Pat agreed. "Though I'm starting to think that Dirty Gertie is right – this trail business is in our heads."

"Maybe she just *wants* us to think that," said Bo. "I think we should ignore her and zip down that chute. We might find the F.B.I.'s secret lair!" She waved to the guards as she sat in the chute. "Is it OK to explore down here?"

"A-OK, ma'am," the guards called back. "Everything's fine."

"Not very bothered, are they?" Pat remarked.

"Don't knock it!" With a grin, Bo launched herself headfirst down the steel tube. "Geroni-*moooooo!*"

Heart pounding, Pat swung himself inside after her. "*Whooaaa!*" he cried, eyes wide as he whizzed down the dark tunnel ... and then landed with a bump on a hard floor.

"What took you so long?" Bo was already exploring their surroundings — a large square room full of funny couches. One doorway led to a small bathroom. Bo poked about in there while Pat investigated an equally tiny kitchen area.

"Hey, look here on the floor," he said "More of those filings!"

Bo studied his find and then looked up. "I wonder . . ." She crossed to a tall

cupboard – the only free-standing furniture in sight – and shunted it aside to reveal a large hole in the wall. "Aha! Unless they have really big mice around here, this must be a secret tunnel. Let's explore!"

"I suppose you're right." Pat frowned. "But if the F.B.I.'s agents have been coming and going through that steel chute on the surface, how come none of the guards outside have noticed?"

"Who cares? *We've* noticed." Bo ducked inside. "Hmm, I smell cowpats. We're on the right track!"

"I wish we knew what the F.B.I. is up to, here in 1969," Pat murmured. "Why do they need the professor's ZEN-generator?"

Bo shrugged. "It makes special magic holes in the ground, doesn't it? Maybe that's what they used to build this tunnel."

"Could be," Pat agreed. "I wonder

where it leads?"

"My luminous udder will light the way!" Bo moved cautiously into the gloom and Pat started after her. "No," she told him. "You wait here in case anyone tries to sneak up behind us. If I find anything, I'll come straight back."

Pat nodded, watching as Bo's glowing udder bobbed away like a lantern.

Further and further along the dark passage she went . . .

Then, suddenly, he heard her startled
voice. "You again!"

Pat gasped. In the eerie glow of Bo's
udder he could see Dexter the calf
standing on his back legs, blocking her
way. And he wasn't alone. Other calves
were stepping out of the shadows to join
him – proper tough-nuts. A shaggy heifer
. . . a beige bison . . . a white water
buffalo . . . There were maybe twelve of
the young cattle in all.

"Well, well," Dexter snarled. "A nosy

cow has found our hideout. Looks like we'll have to teach her what happens when you stick your nose into F.B.I. business. Right, moon-calves?"

The menacing gang closed in on Bo . . .

Chapter Six

POISON!

Pat automatically started forward to help his sister. But without turning round, she raised a hoof to him, warning him to stay hidden. He hesitated – then shrank back into the shadows.

As the mysterious moon-calves attacked, Bo spun round on one hoof – kicking Dexter, tail-whipping the bison and punching the heifer on the conk. All three were sent crashing against the tunnel walls. But then, to Pat's horror, the water buffalo blasted Bo with a steaming stream of yellow gloop.

A butter bazooka, he thought grimly. Again he started forward to help Bo –

but she turned and fiercely shook her head. *Wait!* she mouthed – as a Jersey calf with a cream-cheese cannon joined the attack, slooshing her with a stinky tidal wave of sludge.

Pat covered his eyes. Much as he hated it, he knew Bo was right – if he went to rescue her now without a plan, he'd soon be overcome too.

"There," said the heifer nastily. "That's put her out of action for a while."

"Let's tell our masters," said Dexter, "so they can decide what to do with her before we go to the Foaming Sea."

As the crowd of cattle moved away, Pat tiptoed over to his poor brave sister.

She lay sprawled in a huge sticky puddle of dairy direness. But to his relief, her eyes were already flickering open. "Get after them, bruv," she whispered. "Find out how many there are and where they're hiding – then get out, quick as you can. Those moon-calves play for keeps."

Pat nodded and slipped out of his jacket. "I'll take off this uniform and my ringblender – then I won't stand out so much. But what about you? If the ter-moo-nators come to get you . . ."

"I'll go and get the professor and some guards," Bo told him. "I'll warn them that this barmy baby army is up to something in the Foaming Sea."

"Wherever *that* is," muttered Pat, passing her his human clothes and his ringblender.

"Go on, get going." Bo gave him a quick hug. "And be careful!"

"You too," Pat told her. Then he crept stealthily away.

Back at Launch Control, McMoo sat at a desk with a dozen pads of paper in front of him. While Blinkenshrink held

meetings with his team of technicians and engineers – ensuring that all was ready for the *Apollo 10* launch – the professor was scribbling wildly, drawing demented diagrams and complex equations with a thick black marker.

"Come on," he muttered to himself. "Work it out – what could those ter-moo-nators be trying to build?"

He heard a heavy stomping noise and looked up to find Gertie Barmer waddling into the busy room. Smoky Joe, the hot papa, was behind her – but Pat and Bo were not.

"Ah, Barmer." Blinkenshrink broke off from his meeting. "Have you found our intruder?"

"No, sir," said Gertie grumpily. "But I've put more guards on the exits and entrances, and I've talked to every man on watch out there. No one's seen a single suspicious thing."

"But, dang it all, they must have seen something!" cried the director. "Or did this intruder go floating over their heads?"

"FLOATING!" boomed McMoo, jumping up. "Blinkenshrink, you're brilliant. That's it! I know what all these stolen parts and components could be used to make. Combine them with 'extra nothingness' from my ZEN-generator and you could make an anti-gravity device!"

Gertie stared blankly. "A what?"

"Gravity is a force," McMoo explained. "It's what keeps our feet on the ground. It's what keeps the moon spinning around the earth, and the planets whizzing around the sun."

"And it's the reason why our Saturn V rockets are so big," added Blinkenshrink. "They have to be strong enough to beat the earth's gravity in order to push our moonships into space."

Gertie grunted. "So what does an anti-gravity wotsit do?"

"It makes something heavy weigh nothing at all," said McMoo.

"And it's impossible," said Blinkenshrink flatly. "It's science fiction. McMoo, you're talking bull."

"Oh, I know *bull*, believe me," said the professor. "And I also know when I'm right. Which is most of the time, and especially now. So if you can't do something helpful like believe me,

70

get me a cup of tea."

"Me?" Blinkenshrink was turning red. "Me, the director of this space centre, get the tea?"

"*I've* brought you a cup, Major-General McMoo," said Smoky Joe, who had been hanging back in silence. "Here."

The director looked ready to explode. "Joe, you're a firefighter! Since when do *you* make the tea?"

"And how come you haven't washed yet?" Gertie demanded. "You've still got poop on your head."

"Don't mind them, Smoky, I'm glad you popped by." The professor took the tea. "Cheers!" He swigged it down in a single gulp – and then clutched at his throat. "*Aaargh!*" Suddenly, his head started spinning. His tum felt full of nails.

"What's wrong?" snarled Barmer. "Did he make it too weak?"

"I think . . . he made it with *poison*!" McMoo fell to his knees and went cross-eyed. "Deadly poison, by the taste of it. If I don't get an antidote . . . I'm finished!"

"Holy guacamole!" Blinkenshrink knelt down beside the wilting professor and stabbed a finger at Smoky Joe. "Barmer, arrest that man!"

"Yes, sir." Barmer grabbed Joe in a bear hug.

"That's fine," Joe murmured, as if in a trance. "Everything's A-OK."

"It is not," the director groaned. "What's the President going to say when he finds that his security inspector's been poisoned at my space base – barely an hour before our moon mission is due to launch? Somebody call an ambulance!"

"No," said McMoo weakly. "I'm staying. Whoever did this *wants* me out of the way. But I must get the antidote. Or the an-*tea*-dote!" He struggled up. "Where's the cafeteria?"

"There's one on the next floor down," said Blinkenshrink.

"Come with me – quick!" The professor lurched away. He almost tumbled down the stairs and nearly collapsed in the corridor, but with a supreme bullish effort he reached the canteen. "Right! You know how you can sometimes solve a problem with brute force?"

Blinkenshrink nodded.

"Well, I intend to solve this problem with *brewed* force – the power of tea, taken to the max!" McMoo grabbed a vast catering urn of hot steaming tea, sniffed it to make sure it was safe, then gulped down litre after litre. "More!" he whispered. "This is good strong stuff. It might just drive out the poison!"

"This is crazy." Blinkenshrink chucked a box of tea bags into another huge urn, then emptied a bottle of milk into it too. "Crazy!"

"But *tea*-licious." McMoo glugged down every last drop of the second batch of hot brown brew, then belched loudly. "And now, if you'll excuse me . . ." He dashed out and vanished into the gents' washrooms.

Blinkenshrink winced to hear a noise like a hosepipe squirting enough water to fill a swimming pool — then the flush of a toilet.

Finally, the professor emerged, looking a little brighter. "I think . . . my an–tea–dote worked!"

"You could've died," the director said grimly.

"True," said McMoo, "but still, all that tea — what a way to go!"

"Well, I'm heading back upstairs." Blinkenshrink rushed away. "For crying out loud, I've got a rocket launch to look after!"

"And I've got Pat and Bo," McMoo muttered. "Where are they?" Still feeling a little wobbly, he followed the director out. "Something must be about to happen — something that the F.B.I. don't want me to see. But *what*?"

Chapter Seven

DEADLY DISCOVERIES

In the mysterious tunnels beneath the moon mission's launch pad, Pat could hear voices up ahead. He held his breath as he rounded the corner and found himself in a large cavern lit by lanterns.

A low mooing murmur of voices sounded from inside.

Quickly, Pat concealed himself among some strange quilted suits hanging from pegs on the wall so that he could peep out safely.

With a shiver, he saw that T-207 and T-312 were standing in front of a ramshackle cylinder as big as a bus; it was made of mashed-up metal plates and countless spare parts. Inside, it was crammed with controls – including the yellow lever from the ZEN-generator.

Dexter, the shaggy heifer, the beige bison, the water buffalo – and eight other moon-calves – were gathered around the gigantic tin can.

"We got the milk-cow good, masters," said Dexter.

"She will make a useful slave," grated T-312. "Fetch her."

The water buffalo bowed his outrageous horns and ran off. Pat hoped his sister was safely out of harm's way by now.

T-207 smiled. "Now that Dexter has brought us the final components, our anti-gravity device works perfectly." He started to hang small silver rings at regular intervals around the outside of the canister. "We are ready to launch our mission to the Foaming Sea."

"Ringblenders . . ." Pat realized. Below them, he noticed that four large silver platters had also been attached to the bodywork, connected to each other by

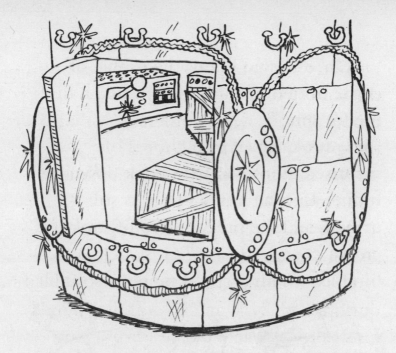

glowing wires. "And F.B.I. time transporters too. They can't be there just for
decoration. What's going on?"

"Let us proceed," said T–312. "By now,
Professor Angus McMoo will be in no
fit state to warn the humans of our
activities."

Why not? thought Pat anxiously. Then
he froze as T–207 seemed to point right
at him.

"Put on your spacesuits," rasped the
ter–moo–nator.

"Uh-oh," said Pat as the rabble of cattle trotted towards him. "They'll find me for sure!"

He broke cover to a chorus of surprised moos and sped back down the tunnel. But the Jersey calf was still armed, and she fired a salvo of stinking cream cheese. *SPLATT!* It struck Pat's hind legs. With a cry of pain, he stumbled

and fell. Then the beige bison charged, horns lowered and ready to gore – but Pat hurled himself aside just in time, and the bison crashed into the wall.

The evil heifer was next into the

attack. But she skidded in the puddle of steaming cheese and collapsed, tripping the bison, who was following just behind. Pat flipped himself back upright – just as T–207 fired a laser and blasted chunks out of the rocky tunnel roof. Stone splinters stung Pat's hide, but he raced on through the choking dust – until, *BANG!* He collided with the returning water buffalo's humungous horns. Head spinning like a butter churn, Pat crumpled to the ground.

"Well done, Waldo," buzzed T–207.

Waldo the water buffalo looked pleased with himself. "I was just running back here to say – the milk-cow's disappeared."

Dexter looked cross. "She got away?"

"Ha!" said Pat weakly. "She's tougher than you thought."

"It does not matter that she has gone," said T–312, marching over. "This bullock will become our slave instead – and a useful hostage. Should any more C.I.A. agents try to stop us, he will suffer!"

Still feeling groggy, McMoo marched into the Launch Control Centre, where Blinkenshrink was shouting orders at his busy engineers. The professor made a beeline for Smoky Joe and Barmer.

"How's my poisoner?" he enquired.

"Everything's A-OK," Joe said happily.

"He won't stop saying that," the burly woman grumbled. "Come to think of it, all the folk out there on patrol have been saying the same thing." She turned up her big nose. "And he still stinks of cow doo-doo."

McMoo plucked a small dollop of brown from Joe's hair. "Hmm, iron filings . . ."

"Your lieutenants found a bunch of those outside near the launch pad," said Gertie. "How'd they wind up in that cow's muck?"

"Perhaps to stick them in place? I wonder . . ." The professor picked up a plastic cup of water from a nearby desk and dropped the muck inside. With a sizzly bang, it went up in smoke.

Gertie coughed. "What the heck—?"

"Just as I thought. No ordinary iron filings." McMoo peered down at the frazzled remains in the water. "Those Fed-up Bulls are masters of mind control. They've brainwashed humans in the past with special swords and dodgy dung beetles — but I've never seen anything like this! The technology must be tiny . . ."

"Are you ever gonna start talking sense?" Gertie grumbled.

"I think these tiny bits of metal are little transmitters sending a special signal," McMoo explained. "That's why none of your guards or the other workers have seen any intruders come or go. The signal makes them believe everything's all right . . . Even when they *see* someone who shouldn't be there, they don't raise the alarm. But because they wanted Joe to do something really bad, they had to give him a more powerful dose of brainwashing – so they glued the transmitters to his head with dung."

"Hogwash!" Gertie grunted. "I dunno what's really going on, but I'm betting it's down to those dang Russians!"

"I almost wish you were right," said McMoo. "But the brains behind these tiny transmitters are far more dangerous . . ."

Suddenly, the door was thrown open – and a bedraggled Little Bo staggered in, supported by two straining guards.

"Bo!" McMoo gasped. As he helped her to sit down, he saw that she was clutching Pat's uniform and ringblender.

"What happened? Where's Pat?"

"The ter-moo-nators have got a
whole bunch of evil nippers working for
them," Bo whispered in his ear. "They're
hiding out in some tunnels underneath
the launch pad. Pat went after them to
find out more."

"Brave, but stupidly dangerous,"
McMoo cried. "We've got to get after
him . . . Er, Bo? What is it?"

Bo was looking past him, her eyes

almost out on stalks. She pointed with a wavering hoof to the huge windows with their perfect view of *Apollo 10*. "Look . . ."

The professor whirled round. "Goodness *moo*," he breathed. "I don't believe it . . . !"

Slowly, silently, a cloud of black smoke was engulfing the spaceship. Then the haze faded to reveal a giant metal canister balanced on top of it! Even from this distance, McMoo could see the silver circles gleaming on the sides of the canister – F.B.I. time machines, linked together to transport the enormous contraption from its hiding place under the ground to its new position up on high . . .

"So *that's* what the ter-moo-nators didn't want me to see," McMoo realized. "The F.B.I. have built a portable HQ – and *Apollo 10*'s going to carry it into space. They're hitching a ride to the moon!"

How do I get out of this one? thought Pat, trapped inside the ter–moo–nators' giant tin can. He'd been tied up, squashed into a strange spacesuit and stuck to the wall with Velcro. The  other moon-calves were bunched up beside him in their own stick-on suits, while most of the available space was given over to sacks and crates and boxes bulging with unknown contents.

"Flight successful," droned T-312.

"We have landed safely," T-207 agreed. Both ter-moo-nators stood on the steel floor of the capsule. The ZEN-generator's yellow lever protruded from a small console at T-207's side.

As a cloud of dark smoke faded from

the thick glass windows, Pat saw that the view was the same as that from the Saturn V's service tower. "We're on top of the rocket," he realized with a thrill of fear. "We could fall off at any moment!"

"Negative," droned T–312. "Our capsule is magnetized to the human spaceship."

"Well, that explains those chalk markings we found on *Apollo 10*," said Pat. "You were measuring the spaceship to be sure you could land on it!"

"Clever, isn't he," sneered Dexter the calf.

"Not clever enough to work out why you're doing all this," Pat admitted.

"Because we must reach the Foaming Sea," rasped T–312. "Our plans depend on it."

"I don't know where that is, but all this stuff you're bringing must weigh hundreds of tons," Pat said. "The rocket will never be able to lift this and *Apollo 10*."

"Negative," said T-207. "Professor McMoo's ZEN-generator is powering an anti-gravity device. This capsule weighs nothing."

"And everything inside it has been placed in a zone of extra nothingness," T-312 added. "Completely weight-free."

"Very clever," said Pat. "But don't you think that Launch Control and all the TV cameras watching will spot this enormous great tin on top of their rocket?"

T-312 shook his gleaming head. "We have placed power-boosted ringblenders all around the capsule. Just as they disguise cattle, so they will disguise our technology."

"Time to blastoff – nine minutes," said T-207. "Our plans have worked perfectly. This time we cannot fail!"

Chapter Eight

BLASTOFF BEDLAM

Over at Launch Control, while dozens of engineers stared at their screens checking system after system, McMoo and Bo were still transfixed by the sight of the F.B.I. space capsule.

"Blinkenshrink!" McMoo yelled. "Call off the countdown. You can't send that rocket into space."

The director looked at him like he was crazy. "What's wrong?"

McMoo pointed through the window. "Can't any of you see that dirty great thing sitting on top of your spaceship?"

"That poison's turned your head funny," said Blinkenshrink. "There's

nothing there. Now, stop distracting me
– every second is crucial."

"I don't think *any* human will be able
to see that thing, Prof." Bo had borrowed
some binoculars and was staring through
them intently. "There are ringblenders all
around it, and—" She gasped. "Oh, no.
Look through the window!"

McMoo grabbed the binoculars. "Bless
my parsnips, Pat's on board that thing!"

"And so are all those cruel cattle kids
who duffed me up," cried Bo. "We've got
to get Pat out of there!"

"We're three miles away and there's
less than eight minutes to go till blastoff,"
McMoo reminded her. "We'd never reach
it in time."

Blinkenshrink had overheard. "I forbid
you to even try," he said sternly. "I don't
care if the President *did* send you, *I* am
running this show. Barmer, make sure
they stay here."

Gertie grinned. "It'll be a pleasure, sir."

"Out of my way!" Bo shouted, raising a hoof, "or I'll whop you into orbit myself."

But as she lunged forward, Gertie moved with surprising speed and sat down on her! The big woman's wobbling bottom crushed the startled milk-cow against the tiled floor. "M-*ooooof*!" she gasped. "Professor, help!"

"Our only chance is to make these people see what's sitting on top of *Apollo 10*," cried McMoo, grabbing assorted

tools from an engineer's desk. "Then
they'll *have* to call off the launch." He
produced Pat's ringblender and set about
it with a scalpel. "If I can only rewire this
thing, we can use it to reverse the illusion
created by the F.B.I.'s ringblenders."

"Well, go on then!" said Bo helplessly.

She watched as McMoo cut open the
silver ring, exposing wires and circuits.
He worked frantically. The flight team
performed their final checks. The clock
went on ticking towards the spaceship's
launch at 16.49.

"T-minus sixty seconds and counting,"
announced Blinkenshrink.

"No more tea, thanks." McMoo froze.
"Oh. You meant T for take-off, didn't
you?"

"T-minus fifty seconds," the director
continued. "Full internal power
transferred to launch vehicle. Looking
good."

"Looking really, really bad, you

mean!" Bo wriggled helplessly beneath the weight of Gertie's bottom. "Come *on*, Professor!"

"*T-minus thirty seconds . . .*"

McMoo worked like a demon. Bo could practically see the steam coming out of his ears. "There!" He hopped up. "That's the rewiring done. Now, if I can just project the anti-illusion beam over to the launch pad . . ."

"*T-minus fifteen seconds, guidance is now internal . . .*"

The professor held the ringblender to the window.

"Why isn't it working?" Bo mooed in despair.

"The power's still building!" McMoo shook the silver ring as the countdown reached nine and the rocket jets blasted into life. "Everybody look at the launch pad!" he bellowed. "LOOK!"

Suddenly, the top of the rocket seemed to blur – and dozens of shocked gasps went up from the watching engineers as the F.B.I. capsule became visible. McMoo and Bo's true appearance became apparent too – but nobody noticed. The spectacle on the launch pad held the whole room transfixed as a crazy chorus of cries almost drowned out the roar of the thrusters:

"*What's that?*"

"*Impossible!*"

"*Something's stuck on the rocket!*"

"Told you so!" Bo wailed.

"But it's too late to abort the countdown," cried Blinkenshrink. "We have liftoff!"

"Nooooooooooooooooo!" wailed McMoo.

Everyone stared in wonder as the

rocket slowly pulled away from the launch pad in a staggering storm of fire and smoke. The giant capsule stayed glued to its top as it tore through the blue afternoon sky and vanished into the clouds.

Then – *PHIZZZ!* Pat's power-boosted ringblender burned out, and the illusion conjured by McMoo and Bo's own ringblenders began to work again.

"Hey!" Gertie was looking down at Bo, shaken. "For a moment there, girlie, I could've sworn you were a cow."

"I could've sworn you were an elephant," Bo retorted. "You both weigh the same. Get off me!"

"Yes, Barmer, stop sitting on the lieutenant," said Blinkenshrink quickly. "It seems you two were right about that thing."

"My poor brother's on board!" wailed Bo.

The professor patted her on the shoulder.

"We'll get him back somehow. The ter-moo-nators must want him alive, or they wouldn't have taken him with them."

"I don't understand any of this!" Blinkenshrink said miserably. "What *was* that thing?"

"I think it was a kind of space capsule," said McMoo.

"Are you sure it wasn't a boat?" asked Bo. "The miserable lumps who clobbered me said it was going to the Foaming Sea—"

"What?" The director turned pink. "But . . . the Foaming Sea is on the moon."

"Of course," breathed McMoo. "There are lots of 'seas' there – not real seas, of course, just sort of plains on the moon's surface."

Blinkenshrink nodded. "When we launch *Apollo 11* in July, she's due to land quite close to the Foaming Sea, in the Sea of Tranquillity . . ."

"Professor," hissed Bo, tugging on his sleeve. "Back in our own time, those same ter-moo-nators attacked us from outer space — remember? This must be how it happens. We haven't been able to stop them at all."

"I'm not ready to give up yet," McMoo told her. "We must find out more about the ter-moo-nators' plans. And I know just who to ask." He dashed over to the snoring firefighter. "Smoky Joe!"

"But he's in that stupid trance," said Gertie.

"True. And to wake someone from a hypnotic state can be dangerous — it should always be done slowly and very, very gently." McMoo frowned. "Still, time is short — so I'll just try conking him on the head with a saucer."

CRASH! The saucer broke on Joe's mucky bonce and he jumped up at once. "Urgh . . . I had a bad dream

where this evil calf was telling me that
if a guy called McMoo turned up with a
couple of friends, I needed to put special
poison in their tea . . ." He gasped as he
saw the professor. "Hey, it's you! You
were in my dream!"

"That wasn't a dream, it really
happened," McMoo told him. "You were
hypnotized. Now, did that evil calf say
anything else?"

"Uh-huh. He was quite a show-off."
Joe shivered. "He said that fed-up bulls
would take over the moon — and start a
terrible war that would destroy the
human race!"

"Space bulls?" Gertie snorted.
"Hogwash!"

"This threat is real," McMoo insisted.
"They have incredible technology. You
saw the way they hid their capsule in
plain sight on top of your spacecraft!"

Blinkenshrink buried his head in his
hands. "How can we
stop this madness? If
the press find out
we've accidentally
sent evil bulls into
space — that our
moon missions
may have doomed
the world . . ."

"No one must know," said McMoo.
"You must send a top-secret mission to

the moon to defeat these mad bulls, using extra-specially secret astronauts."

Blinkenshrink blinked. "Like who?"

"Me and Bo, of course!" McMoo grinned. "The sooner we leave the planet, the sooner we can save it. Let's go!"

Chapter Nine

LUNAR-SEA!

Strapped into her seat in the cramped moonship, Bo surveyed the squillions of switches and dials all around her. She was a brave cow, but right now the butterflies in her stomach felt more like blackbirds.

Here she was, about to be launched into space!

"Professor," she said. "How did you ever persuade Blinky and his team to let a couple of untrained chancers like us fly a thirty-billion-dollar spaceship?"

"I had some electronic help." McMoo, in the seat beside her, smiled ruefully. "I found some of those iron filings in one of

the pockets in Pat's uniform and fiddled around a bit."

Bo gave him a sharp look. "You hypnotized everyone?"

"Only a bit!" McMoo protested. "They don't mind. Listen." He flicked a switch. "Blinkenshrink, this is *Apollo 10½*. Are we OK to launch?"

"Everything's fine," the director said happily.

"See?" McMoo's smile faded. "We're still trying to keep history on the right track, remember? The world at large didn't see the F.B.I. riding *Apollo 10* – and anyone watching our rocket launch will think it's just a test."

"I just hope we can stop the ter-moo-nators," said Bo.

"That's what we're aiming for," agreed McMoo. "Well, that and the moon!"

"Starting countdown," said Blinken-shrink. "*T-minus ninety seconds . . .*"

Bo gulped. Sweating in her spacesuit, she ticked off the seconds while McMoo flicked switches and checked instruments.

"One thing you should know, Bo," said the professor. "I've had a fiddle with the fuel mix of this rocket so it'll go a lot faster. It's our only chance of catching up with *Apollo 10* . . . but it does mean we're going to be accelerating at over 35,000 miles per hour."

"Bring it on," Bo growled. "I'll grin

and bear it. Or grin and *cow* it, anyway!"
She looked across at the empty seat
beside McMoo. "Hang in there, Pat.
We're coming to get you!"

McMoo winked at her as the
spaceship rumbled and the rocket's
engines fired. "*Three . . . two . . . one . . .
we have liftoff!*"

The rocket blasted away, shooting into
the sky like some phenomenal firework.
Bo found herself crushed back into her
seat with the force. Her eyes felt like

they were being squashed into her brain and she could barely breathe.

"Here we go!" cried McMoo, working the vital controls. Then the launch rocket fell away in stages, leaving the little craft to travel on alone through the cold, endless darkness of space . . .

The journey to the moon had begun!

Long empty hours turned to longer, emptier days as the three spaceships travelled on through the infinite blackness – *Apollo 10*, *Apollo 10½* and the F.B.I. capsule.

The astronauts on board *Apollo 10* performed their duties with no idea that they were carrying evil bull-creatures on their roof. There was nothing they could do about it in any case, so Blinkenshrink had kept the news quiet.

Slowly, the disc of the earth dwindled, and the grey, pockmarked bulk of the moon grew larger.

On the F.B.I. ship, Pat tossed and turned but could not sleep. He had never felt more afraid – trapped in a tin can hurtling through the deadly vacuum of space, with only his worst enemies for company. He was grateful for the special spacesuit he was wearing that sucked away his poo and wee without him needing to move.

But on *Apollo 10½*, McMoo and Bo had no such luxury.

"Space travel stinks," said Bo, watching miserably as one of her cowpats floated in the zero gravity.

"I hear the toilets on the space shuttle in the 1980s are much better," the professor said cheerily.

"Earth to *Apollo 10½ ...*" Blinkenshrink's voice crackled through the ship's speakers. "You have made

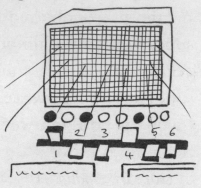

incredible time. You have overtaken *Apollo 10* and should reach the Foaming Sea in one hour."

"So, tell me, Prof," said Bo. "What's your plan for dealing with the F.B.I. when we haven't got any weapons?"

"Er . . . let's worry about that *after* we've reached the moon, shall we?" McMoo looked shifty. "Now, *Apollo* space missions usually have a three-man crew – one astronaut stays in the mother ship while two take the 'lunar taxi' to the surface of the moon." He wiped a bit of muck off a small metal box. "Still, hopefully my homemade remote control will do the business."

"We've done enough 'business' in here," said Bo, holding her nose. "Let's get going!"

Just seventy miles from the moon, McMoo put *Apollo 10½* into lunar orbit. Then, he and Bo changed into thick, extra-padded spacesuits and special helmets for the final stage of their epic voyage. They crawled into the lunar taxi that would take them to the surface, and broke away from the mother ship. Carefully, using short bursts of jet power to control their flight, the lunar taxi descended towards the barren grey desert of the moon. Closer it came. Closer and closer, until at last . . .

Touchdown!

Bo felt a thrill of wonder as McMoo opened the door onto a whole new world. For billions of years the moon had shone in the sky, but the idea of reaching it had seemed an impossible dream — until now.

"Well, we did it . . ." McMoo hesitated in the doorway. "I suppose I should say it's a small step for a bull — but a giant leap for cowkind!"

"You should," Bo agreed, "if you want to send everyone to sleep. Me, *I'm* going to say — *Wheeeeee!*" She jumped down, falling surprisingly slowly in the moon's low gravity. "We're the first cows on the mooooooo-n!"

But then she looked up into the black sky, where the earth hung among the stars like a bright blue eye, and gasped.

A gigantic tin can was glinting in the starlight above — and heading straight for them!

Pat's stomach was performing backflips as the F.B.I. prepared for landing.

The ter-moo-nators' technology had performed perfectly so far. As *Apollo 10* had neared the moon, a flick of a switch had reversed the capsule's magnets and flipped it free. The human astronauts never noticed a thing; they flew around the moon and then headed back to earth, their mission a success but uneventful – or so they thought.

But the F.B.I. mission was just getting started. All that remained for the ter-moo-nators to achieve was a lunar touchdown . . .

But to Pat's incredulous delight, it seemed he might have some hope of rescue after all. Another *Apollo* ship was already parked proudly in the moondust, and two spacesuited figures stood beside it.

Pounding parsnips! Pat thought. *I'd recognize those two anywhere, even in space helmets. It's—*

"C.I.A. agents McMoo and Bo Vine

sighted!" droned T-312.

The rabble of moon-calves mooed and grunted in disgust and dismay.

"Impossible!" rasped T-207, his horns quivering. "McMoo cannot have arrived before us."

"But he has!" cried Pat triumphantly. "The C.I.A. will always be one giant step ahead of you."

Dexter scowled at Pat. "Squash them, masters!"

"Splatter them!" added Waldo the water buffalo. "Grind them into moondust!"

"Preparing to land," T-207 rumbled. "Right on top of the C.I.A. scum!"

Chapter Ten

BATTLE BY EARTHLIGHT

"Take cover, Bo!" McMoo ordered as the capsule swooped down overhead. He knew that, on the moon, gravity was one-sixth that of earth's – which meant that they could leap six times as far! With a massive bounce, he somersaulted through the air, and Bo tumbled after him – just as the F.B.I. capsule landed beside them in a spectacular cloud of dust.

Bo landed on her back, scraping her suit on rough moon rock.

"Careful!" McMoo commanded, landing on one hand and cartwheeling onto his back legs. "One tear in your

astronaut gear and your air will escape
– it'll be game over!"

"I'm all right," Bo assured him. "But
how are we going to stop the ter-moo-
nators and their little helpmates when
they outnumber us seven to one?"

"You *cannot* stop us!" roared T-207,
kicking open the door to the capsule
and stamping outside. He was wearing
a space helmet that barely contained

his silver horns – as was T-312, looming just behind him, his laser weapon primed for firing.

"You were fools to come here," T-207 continued. "Now you will be ter-moo-nated."

A blast of green laser-light shot from T-312's wrist. McMoo dived aside and the moon rock behind him exploded in a storm of fragments. Thinking fast, he caught a stone and hurled it at T-312, catching him right on the space helmet.

The ter-moo-nator's eyes glowed angry red. "You will surrender at once."

"No way, beef-cheeks!" Bo shouted, throwing another chunk of rock at T-207. "We'll go on fighting till you give us back my brother!"

"Here he is!" snarled Dexter, flinging the tied-up Pat out through the capsule's door. Pat landed with a muffled crunch. "Surrender now – or we take off his space helmet."

"Yeah!" yelled the beige bison, following Dexter out. "Let's see how long he lasts with no air!"

The other young cattle filed out of the capsule. Waldo the water buffalo was carrying two sacks labelled GRAIN, while the heifer held a crate of  drilling equipment. "Kill them all now," she snarled. "We've got an underground base to build."

"No, wait!" McMoo held up his hooves. "We surrender. Just do us a favour before you squish us, will you? Tell us why Dexter is wearing a perfect replica of a *Russian* spacesuit!"

Bo frowned and looked at Dexter more closely. Sure enough, his suit was slightly different, with red strips along the arms, and badges in funny writing.

"Very well," said T-207. "Because—"

"Oh, and can you also tell us why you want to build an underground base just here?" McMoo added.

T-207 tried again. "Sensors show this area is rich in certain minerals which—"

"And what's all this about starting a terrible war among the humans?" Bo asked.

"Yes, how *will* you do that?" Pat demanded, straining against the ropes that bound him.

"WE ARE TRYING TO TELL YOU," boomed T-312. "When the first American humans land on the moon in two months' time - on the twentieth of July 1969 – we will be here to greet them. We will wear ringblenders and dress as Russian astronauts."

Bo frowned. "You want the Americans

to think that their biggest rivals got to the moon ahead of them?"

"Yes," said T-207. "And then the 'Russians' will ter–moo–nate the US astronauts!"

"That's horrible." McMoo was appalled. "Why would you ever do such a thing?"

"The moon landing will be shown on live TV all over the world," said Dexter. "When our masters squish those astronauts, over five hundred million humans will be watching."

"There will be outrage," hissed T-207. "Accusations. Denials. Threats. Counter threats."

"Finally," gloated T-312, "fear and hate between the Americans and the Russians will lead to all-out war."

McMoo nodded grimly. "A nuclear war that will leave the earth a radioactive wasteland."

"You're loonies!" Bo shouted. "You'll

be killing millions of cows as well as humans."

"And the earth will take ages to recover," said Pat.

"*We* won't care," sneered Dexter. " We'll be safe up here on the moon."

"We've brought all the things we need to build an underground moon base," bragged the heifer. "The rocks in the Foaming Sea are rich in iron; we'll use it to build lots of super-weapons."

"And we'll plant special twenty-sixth-century crops that grow anywhere." Waldo waved his sack of grain. "Even in moon soil."

The beige bison nodded. "We'll even recycle our wee and use it as water."

"Remind me never to come for tea," said McMoo. "I suppose that by the time the radiation's faded, you young cattle will have grown up."

"We'll be in our prime," said Dexter, flexing his muscles.

"And the ter-moo-nators will build us a spaceship so we can travel back to earth," said  the heifer happily. "We'll be the first of a new master race of cows!"

"And any surviving humans will be ter-moo-nated." T-207's voice rose in pitch and power. "The age of the Clever Cow will begin in the 1970s – almost six hundred years ahead of schedule. And the F.B.I. will rule victorious for all time!"

"There's something I don't understand," said Pat, still trying to free himself. "Why did you need to hitch a ride with *Apollo 10*? Surely you could've taken a spaceship from the future and brought it back through time."

T-207 scowled. "It is true that in our own time, a huge lunar base covers this part of the moon. Cow scientists work there side-by-side with the hated humans on a new space programme."

"But we could not have stolen their technology without alerting the entire C.I.A.," said T-312. "They would have sent an army of agents to stop us. So instead we have been super-sneaky."

"That's for sure," agreed McMoo. "And you've beaten us completely. The C.I.A. will be furious." He gave Pat a knowing look. "Perhaps we should be given the *sack*."

"Once we have changed history by starting this war, the C.I.A. will no longer exist," hissed T-312. "Its founder, Madame Milkbelly, will never be born."

"That's *sack*-rilege!" McMoo was now looking between Pat and Waldo. Pat got the feeling the professor was trying to tell him something. "I mean, it goes against the *grain* . . ."

Pat gasped as he realized McMoo was trying to draw his attention to the water buffalo's sacks of grain – and guessed the professor's plan. He finally untied the ropes that held him and mouthed to Bo, *Get ready*.

"I think they're up to something," said Dexter. "Let's get rid of them now before they—"

"SACK ATTACK!" yelled Pat,

grabbing a rock and hurling it at one of the bulging bags. It tore a hole in the sack, and suddenly a storm of grain erupted from inside, swirling like smoke in the low gravity, blinding the mooncalves and their masters.

At the same time, Bo did a hundstand and booted T-207 with both hooves right in his space helmet. He flew backwards into the bison and Waldo, and accidentally tore the second bag of grain open too.

As the seeds swarmed through the air like a smokescreen, Pat and McMoo charged T-312. The metal monster never saw them coming. Pat's hooves whumped him in the guts and McMoo kicked his legs out from under him. T-312 was sent spiralling through space and crash-landed in a bowl-shaped dip in the ground.

"From ter-moo-nator to ter-moo-*crater*," cried McMoo, high-fiving Pat.

"That joke was rubbish," Bo complained, swinging Waldo round and round by his space helmet.

"Let's hear you do better." Pat ducked as Dexter fired thick yellow spray from his bazooka. "Or do I mean *butter*?"

"All right, try this gag for size," said Bo, still wielding the water buffalo. "Why not visit my cattle-*club* – I think it'll be a *HIT*!" She swung Waldo's legs into the beige bison's back, smashing him down into the dust. As the Jersey calf came at

Bo with a cream-cheese cannon, she struck again with her living bat, dealing her attacker a bone-jarring blow.

"Your club's a knockout," said Pat approvingly, belly-slapping Dexter against the side of the F.B.I. ship.

"Don't get cocky," McMoo warned his friends, just as T-312 emerged from his crater – and fired his laser straight at Bo. *KER-ZIZZZ!*

The energy bolt blasted a hole in her spacesuit's backpack and sent her tumbling to her knees . . .

Chapter Eleven

'AIR-RAISING!

"Noooooo!" Pat shouted, horrified.
"Little Bo!"

"I'll deal with metal-mush – you
check she's all right." McMoo leaped
thirty metres through the air and brought
his butt bumping down on T-312's head,
pounding him into the ground. "Well?"

"The laser hit her air supply," cried
Pat. "All her oxygen is escaping."

"But these cow-creeps and bull-bullies
won't be escaping *me!*" Bo vowed, taking
off like a jet plane and whizzing over the
lunar surface. "*Wa-hoooo!*"

"Bo!" Pat gasped. "You're flying!"

"It's the air rushing out of her

backpack," McMoo realized. "It's pushing her along like a rocket's jets!"

"Or like a guided *moo*-sile!" Bo dive-bombed the remaining cattle. "Ha!"

"Their spacesuits, Bo!" yelled McMoo, suddenly inspired. "Make holes in their spacesuits!"

Bo started tugging at the thick material of the moon-calves' protective clothing. "That's *torn* it!"

Dexter squealed, dropping his bazooka. "There's a hole in my spacesuit!"

"Mine too!" sobbed the heifer. "We'll freeze! We'll suffocate!"

"Help! Moomy!" A young Texas Longhorn bull tried to dodge the flying Bo, but she was too speedy, grabbing his oxygen tank and yanking it off.

"Cheers, steak-chops!" she cried. "I'll be needing to top up my air if I keep shooting about like this."

"Return to the capsule, children," T-207 warbled. "There is air inside."

But Pat and the professor had already leaped forward to slam the capsule door shut, blocking the cattle's escape – even as Bo attacked the others, snatching at *their* spacesuits before retreating out of reach.

"Ha!" she cried. "Not so tough now, are you?"

T-207 jumped up and made a grab for Bo – just as T-312 tried once more to fry her with his laser! The blast meant for Bo ended up scorching T-207's left leg and knocking him into a boulder. He bounced off it and rebounded back into his fellow ter-moo-nator.

"Help!" wailed Waldo, trying to hold a split in his suit together with both hooves. "Help us, somebody!"

"Certainly!" McMoo jumped up and grabbed two of the plate-like portable time transporters jammed on the side of the capsule, twisting them free. "If you travel back to your own time, six hundred years from now, you'll be safe – because this area will be covered by a C.I.A. moon base, right?"

"That's what the ter-moo-nator said," Pat agreed, heaving with all his might on the third and fourth time transporters glued to the F.B.I. capsule on the opposite side. "There'll be lots of lovely air to breathe. And hopefully lots of prison cells too."

"Mission abort!" mooed the moon-calves, scrambling onto the silver platters in threes. "Abort!"

"Wait," T-312 roared, his metal limbs still tangled with T-207's. "You are taking all available time transporters . . . Your masters will be left marooned!"

"Good!" mooed Dexter. "We wanted to be all-conquering cattle . . . but you've messed everything up!"

Clouds of smoke as black as the skies above wafted up from the time transporters . . .

Then the moon-calves were gone.

"We did it!" cried Pat. "Twelve down
– that's evened the odds."

Bo landed beside him with a bump,
and McMoo quickly replaced her
emptying oxygen tank with the one
she'd whipped off Waldo. The two
ter-moo-nators, looking battered
and bruised, were clambering up
once again.

"Now to finish off those robo-bull
buttheads," Bo growled.

"Just as soon as I've got my ZEN-
generator out of their ship." McMoo
opened the capsule door and ducked
inside. "Bo, remember you said it would
be good for clobbering people? I aim to
put it to the test . . ."

"Do not remove the generator," T-312
commanded. "The systems are still live.
There will be energy feedback into the
local environment."

Bo frowned. "What's he on about?"

Suddenly, a huge, colourful explosion burst out of the bottom of the F.B.I. capsule. Pat and Bo were flung forward by invisible shockwaves as a huge split opened up in the moon's surface, spitting geysers of rock and dust high into the air . . .

"I'm guessing *that*'s what he's on about," cried Pat.

"And I really should've listened!" McMoo tumbled out of the capsule with the yellow lever and its throbbing metal box. "Now runaway ZEN-energy is opening and closing magic holes in the moon's crust . . ." The huge split in the seething lunar surface suddenly sealed over – before ripping itself apart all over again. "See what I mean?"

"No!" yelled Pat. "My eyes are closed!"

"We've got to get out of here." Bo clung onto Pat as the F.B.I. capsule fell onto its side, rocking in the shockwaves as ZEN energy sparked in all directions. "Quickly!"

"Our capsule will fall into the extra nothingness," groaned T-312.

"We must stop it," buzzed T-207.

While Pat, Bo and McMoo bounded away towards *Apollo 10½*, the ter-moo-nators charged towards their stricken ship. The capsule was balanced perilously on the edge of the lunar chasm, and Pat watched as the robo-bulls hurled themselves through the open doors . . .

Just as the biggest explosion of energy yet crackled out from inside! The black split in the rock beside it grew wider and darker still, spitting debris high into the sky – before swallowing the ter-moo-nators and their capsule completely. Pat watched in alarm as black nothingness devoured more and more of the surface, reaching out hungrily for the C.I.A. agents and their tiny borrowed spaceship . . .

But at the last moment, like a great dark wave crashing back over the shore, the colossal crack sealed over completely – trapping the ter-moo-nators and their capsule deep beneath the moon's surface.

McMoo kissed the big yellow lever and wiped his brow. "There! The ZEN

energy's been exhausted."

"Leaving the ter–moo–nators trapped deep within the lunar rock," said Pat.

Bo beamed. "So now they can't get out and squish the first *men* on the moon when *Apollo 11* gets here in July!"

"We *WILL* get out." The unearthly rattle of T–312's transmitted voice boomed through the speakers of the cows' helmets. "The capsule and its contents have been buried with us."

"We have tools. Drills. Weapons," T–207 said coldly. "Working at maximum capacity, I calculate we will tunnel our way to the surface in three years, ten months and eleven days."

"As long as that?" A relieved grin crossed McMoo's face. "Well, you won't find many American astronauts to nobble once you're free. Because the *Apollo* moon missions stop in December 1972 – a full *three* months before you can poke out your ugly metal heads!"

"Then . . . we really have won!" Bo cheered. "Yes!"

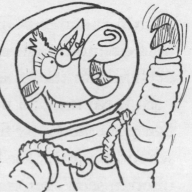

"You *still* will not triumph," rasped T-312. "We will build our moon base as planned, here beneath the ground. We will mine metals from these rocks and build spaceships and weapons. Then we will build robot pilots to fly them to earth and destroy you!"

"Oh yeah?" said McMoo. "And how long is all that going to take?"

"Our computers predict . . . between forty and forty-five years," said T-207. "But we do not tire. We do not give up. Our fleet's first act will be to destroy your farm — and the world will follow!"

There was a click as the ter-moo-nators switched off their transmitters. Then silence, as cold and deep as space.

"Forty to forty-five years from now,"

McMoo muttered. "That means they'll be ready to attack in our own time!"

"That's it, then," said Pat quietly. "We may have stopped the F.B.I.'s first plan. But now we know for sure that their second plan works – because we've already seen them invade the farm."

Bo nodded. "We haven't changed history at all!"

"So it would seem," said McMoo grimly. "And if that's the case, there's only one thing to do – go back to the future and face our fate!"

Chapter Twelve

THE MOON-ROCK FUTURE-SHOCK

Before the C.I.A. agents could face anything, they had to get back to earth. Pat was a lot more squashed on the voyage home, but the company was much better! The human technology worked like a charm, even if the toilets didn't, and after fifty-four hours *Apollo 10½* started its descent through the atmosphere.

"This is the tricky bit," McMoo explained. "Moving through the layers of air in the atmosphere puts a lot of strain on our ship – makes it glow red-hot!"

"Being an astronaut's a tough life,"

Pat mused. "The humans who do it are heroes!"

McMoo looked proudly at his young friends. "And so are the cows and bullocks."

Luckily, *Apollo 10½*'s heat shields held out, and the cramped craft splashed down safely in the Pacific Ocean.

Helicopters collected its unusual crew in utter secrecy and took them to a US navy ship, which transported them to a nearby island where a plane was waiting to carry them back to the Kennedy Space Centre . . .

Pat barely noticed the long journey. All he could think about was the nightmare waiting for them in the twenty-first century: the dented, rusty ter-moo-nators, many decades older, but with their thirst for revenge unquenched . . .

Director Blinkenshrink greeted them warmly upon their arrival back at the Space Centre, and listened to their adventures in amazement.

"You have done America and the world a great service," he declared finally, walking them to Launch Control's exit. "Our astronauts are safe and the *Apollo* moon missions can continue in peace."

"A terrible war has been averted," McMoo agreed. "And since we want to keep all this business secret, I think my lieutenants and I should slip away sharpish, don't you?"

"Yes, please," said Blinkenshrink. "The sooner things get back to normal here, the better."

"Oh, what about Gertie Barmer?" asked Pat. "She knows the truth of everything that happened too."

"She quit her job as security chief," the director revealed. "Said that guarding a space centre was way too much like hard work. She's gone off to marry a rich farmer instead and start a family in the United Kingdom." He shook hands with the C.I.A. agents. "Well, so long . . . and thanks again."

As the big man left, Pat turned to Bo and McMoo. "Ugh!" he cried, horrified. "Gertie must be going off to have Bessie!"

"Euwww!" Bo pulled a face.

"So in a way the F.B.I. are responsible for Bessie Barmer!" McMoo concluded, ushering them away from the Launch Control Centre towards the Time Shed. "And it was because I wanted to escape Bessie that I built my time machine ... Which led in turn to us joining the C.I.A. and becoming the F.B.I.'s biggest enemies." He laughed heartily. "We've defeated them so many times throughout history – and they brought it all down on themselves!"

Bo sighed as he opened the Time Shed's doors. "But now they're going to bring the whole of their rotten fleet down on us."

"Eh? Rotten fleet?" McMoo looked at her, a slow smile spreading over his face. "Yes, of course . . ." He slotted the ZEN-generator back into place in the horseshoe of controls. "Perhaps the future isn't as bleak as we think!"

Pat felt a tiny spark of hope. "What do you mean?"

"I'll show you," McMoo declared. "By landing a split-second after we first departed . . ."

He pulled on the red take-off lever, and Bo frowned as the Time Shed rattled away, fast-forwarding history to take them to the early twenty-first century. "You sure about this, Prof? A split-second after we left, those two ter-moo-nators were about to crash through the—"

BWAMMM!
The doors were
smashed open to
reveal the
battered T-207
and T-312, now
forty-plus years
older. In the
skies above, a dozen Moo-FOs could be
seen, getting closer.

"Stand back, boys." Bo jumped
protectively in front of them. "I'm not
going down without a fight."

"But *they* will," said McMoo with a
grin.

T-312 frowned at him. "Explain."

"Certainly," said McMoo. "You see,
back on the moon, escaping energy from
my ZEN-generator created millions of
magic holes in just about everyone and
everything it touched – including you,
your capsule, the rocks you mined for
metal, the parts you used to make your

robot pilots—"

Suddenly – *BWOOOOM!* A Moo-FO in the sky exploded. Seconds later, another one followed it into fireworks . . . and another!

"Impossible!" roared T-207. "What is happening?"

"Don't you see?" said McMoo. "You've built your whole fleet from unstable materials. It's a miracle you and your ships even made it through the earth's atmosphere! And now, as their heat shields cool down again . . ."

BWAMM! "They're falling to pieces!" Pat laughed as another Moo-FO blew itself apart.

"And now I'm wondering just how tough these old ter-moo-nators are!" Bo charged up to T-207 and hoof-jabbed his chest-plate. *CLUNK! CLANG!* The whole of his armour fell to bits, revealing his skinny grey bull body – and a pair of spotty underpants!

"Urgh!" said Pat. "Get out of my sight!" So saying, he kicked him back out of the Time Shed, where he landed in a heap.

"You will pay for your insolence," snarled T–312, raising his wrist-laser. But as he tried to zap Pat, the blaster backfired and blew his own armour off in a thick cloud of silvery mist.

"No smoking in the shed," cried Bo

cheekily. She butted the dazed bull-bot out through the doors to join T-207, sprawled in the shadow of their ship. Then – *KRANNG!* – the entire Moo-FO crumpled like tin foil and collapsed, before ripping apart with a white-hot *KA-BOOM!*

"Ha-haaa!" cheered the professor as the last of the Moo-FOs exploded in the sky. "So much for the great invasion!"

Pat's face fell. "But what about Bessie and Gertie? They were hiding behind the wall outside."

Bo nodded. "They were ready to knock down our shed before – and after all they've seen tonight . . ."

McMoo had already shrugged off his uniform and whipped out his ringblender, and now stood peering out into the smoke on all fours. "Let's check it out."

Pat ran over, with Bo just behind. He saw that Bessie was staring around in

shock; and Gertie was staring at *her*.

"So," the wobbly old woman snarled.
"As soon as I say I'm thinking of staying,
you stage a big dumb joke like this to try
and scare me off, huh?"

"No, Mum!" Bessie protested. "This
was nothing to do with me."

"Hogwash!" Gertie bellowed. "You
know I hate cows and space more than
anything, so you went and mixed 'em
up halfway through my holiday, just

to freak me out. And it's worked too!"
She lumbered away like a vast, wrinkly
jelly. "Goodbye!"

"Mum! Wait!" shouted Bessie. "Don't
be such an old ratbag."

"Why not?" Gertie shot back. "*You*
are!"

"There we go – all's well that ends
well!" McMoo grinned at his friends.
"There's nothing like an invasion from
space to ruin a neighbourhood's
reputation."

Pat nodded happily. "It doesn't look as
if Gertie will be moooving in just yet."

That moment, a large white crate-like
object appeared in a blaze of light.

McMoo blinked. "It's a C.I.A. time
machine!"

"About *time* our so-called employers
showed their noses," grumbled Bo, "after
letting us do all the work!"

A huge, elderly cow with an udder as
big as a set of bagpipes emerged with a

squad of purple-sashed bodyguards.

"What a day this is turning out to be!" McMoo exclaimed. "It's Madame Milkbelly the Third – Queen of Cows in the twenty-sixth century." He bowed in reverence, and Pat did the same.

"Wotcha, Madame Milky," said Bo, with a clumsy curtsey.

"Greetings to you all," said the grand old cow. "I decided to visit you in person because ten young F.B.I. agents have recently turned up at our moon base in torn spacesuits, complaining about the three of you most bitterly. We tried to contact you . . ."

"Sorry," said McMoo. "The phone packed up and we've been a bit busy . . ."

"So I can see." Madame Milkbelly gestured to her guards, who quickly dragged the broken ter-moo-nators away into custody. "It seems the F.B.I.'s latest time crime went unnoticed by our agency – but you seem to have beaten those wretched bulls once again."

"You know it, your maj." Bo struck a heroic pose. "And it only took us forty-odd years!"

"And now we're back on earth," Pat added, "I'm keeping my hooves firmly on the ground."

"Easier said than done when you're a

star agent of the Cows In Action," said McMoo happily. "I just know there'll soon be another action-packed mission coming our way – and guess how that makes me feel?"

"Don't tell us," laughed Bo, and Pat piped up too: "Over the *mooooon!*"

THE END

will return in

THE VIKING EMOO-GENCY

Visit www.**stevecolebooks**.co.uk for fun, games, jokes, to meet the characters and much, much more!

Welcome to a world where dinosaurs fly spaceships and cows use a time-machine . . .

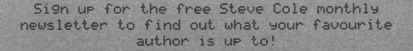

Sign up for the free Steve Cole monthly newsletter to find out what your favourite author is up to!

ALSO BY STEVE COLE

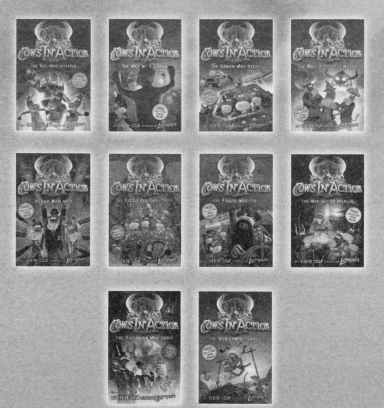

DINOSAURS...
IN SPACE!

**Meet Captain Teggs Stegosaur
and the crew of the amazing spaceship
DSS *Sauropod* as the ASTROSAURS fight
evil across the galaxy!**

IF YOU CAN'T TAKE THE SLIME
DON'T DO THE CRIME!

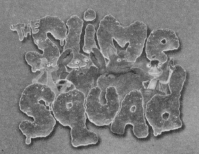

Plog, Furp, Zill and Danjo aren't just
monsters in a rubbish dump. They are
crime-busting super-monsters,
here to save their whiffy world!